tHis BooK BElongs to:

- -

- -

W9-BAH-665

For Alayna, Allyson, and Caroline: wishing you many, many dogs. —SSB

For Mum and Bill, with love. —LH

Copyright © 2010 by Stephanie Stuve-Bodeen 🐾 Illustrations copyright © 2010 by Linzie Hunter

All rights reserved. Except as permitted under the U.S. Copyright Act of 1976, no part of this publication may be reproduced, distributed, or transmitted in any form or by any means, or stored in a database or retrieval system, without the prior written permission of the publisher.

Little, Brown Books for Young Readers
Hachette Book Group 🐾 237 Park Avenue 🐾 New York, NY 10017
Visit our Web site at www.lb-kids.com

Little, Brown Books for Young Readers is a division of Hachette Book Group, Inc.
The Little, Brown name and logo are trademarks of Hachette Book Group, Inc.

First Edition: January 2010

Library of Congress Cataloging-in-Publication Data

Bodeen, S. A. (Stephanie A.), 1965–
A small brown dog with a wet pink nose / by Stephanie
Stuve-Bodeen; [illustrations by Linzie Hunter]. —1st ed.
p. cm.
Summary: Amelia will stop at nothing to convince her parents
to let her adopt a very special dog.
ISBN 978-0-316-05830-8
[1. Dog adoption—Fiction. 2. Dogs—Fiction. 3. Parent and
child—Fiction.] I. Hunter, Linzie, ill. II. Title.
PZ7.B63515Sm 2009
[E]—dc22
2008039298

10 9 8 7 6 5 4 3 2 1

IM 🐾 Printed in Singapore

The illustrations for this book were done digitally.
The text was set in NeutraText and the display type was hand-lettered.

A small BROWN DOG with a WET Pink NOSE

written by
STEPHANIE STUVE-BODEEN

illustrated by
LINZIE HUNTER

LB
LITTLE, BROWN AND COMPANY
New York 🐾 Boston

Amelia wanted a dog. But not just any dog.
Every day she asked her parents,

"May I have a small brown dog with a wet pink nose?"
Every day the reply was the same.

"Oh, no," said Amelia's mother.

Amelia's father added,
"We're just not ready for a dog."

SQUEAK!

SQUEAK!

That didn't stop Amelia from asking,

every day,

just in case they changed their minds.

But one morning, Amelia asked a different question.
"But if we did have a dog, could we name him Bones?"

"Oh, yes," said Amelia's mother.

Amelia's father added, "That's a fine name for a dog."

After breakfast, Amelia asked, "If we did have a dog, could he live with us in our house?"

"Oh, yes," said Amelia's mother.

Amelia's father added, "A dog would be part of the family."

A bit later, on the way to school, Amelia asked another question.

If we had a dog, could he sit by me in the car and look out the window?

"Oh, yes," said Amelia's mother.

Amelia's father added, "That would be a grand place for him to sit."

While Amelia was putting on her shin guards for soccer practice, she asked, "If we had a dog, could I walk him every day?"

"Oh, yes," said Amelia's mother.

Amelia's father added, "Exercise would be very good for him."

During dinner, Amelia looked at her peas and asked, "If we had a dog, could I feed him?"

"Oh, yes," said Amelia's mother.

Amelia's father added, "Feeding a dog is very important."

yuck

That night, Amelia snuggled down in her bed and wiggled her toes. She asked, "If we had a dog, could he sleep with me?"

Just before her parents turned out the light, Amelia asked one more question.

If we did have a dog and he got lost, would we find him and bring him back?

"Oh, yes," said Amelia's mother.

Amelia's father added, "He'd keep your toes warm."

"Oh, yes," said Amelia's mother.

Amelia's father added, "We wouldn't stop looking until we found him."

A few days later, Amelia's mother was standing in the kitchen when Amelia called out,

"Shut the door so Bones won't get out!"

"Who is Bones?" asked Amelia's mother. Amelia smiled.

Our new **dog**. He's small and BROWN with a wet Pink nose.

Amelia's mother did not see a small brown dog with a wet pink nose, but she firmly latched the door anyway.

A bit later, Amelia's father was about to sit in his favorite chair, when Amelia screeched . . .

Our new dog.
He's small and brown
with a wet pink nose.

Amelia's father did not see a
small brown dog with a wet pink nose.
But he sat on the couch instead
of his favorite chair anyway.

All week long, Amelia and Bones did everything together.

1

Bones lived in the house with Amelia and her parents.

2

On the way to school, Bones sat next to Amelia so he could look out the window.

3

Before soccer practice, Amelia walked Bones up and down the sidewalk.

4

During dinner, Amelia shared her food with Bones. (Lucky for her, he loved green vegetables.)

At night, Bones snuggled up next to Amelia
in bed and kept her toes very warm.

Amelia and Bones were very happy.

Until the morning when Amelia's toes were cold when she woke up.

Amelia ran into
the kitchen, sobbing.

"HE'S GONE!"

"Who's gone?" asked Amelia's mother and father at the very same time.

"Bones!" Amelia sniffled. "You promised if we had a dog and he was lost, we'd find him."

"Oh—," started Amelia's mother.

"Well, we—," began Amelia's father.

"Oh, yes. We *did* promise," said Amelia's mother.

Amelia's father added, "Let's go look for Bones."

The family drove around the neighborhood.

Bake Shop

REX

DOG GONE BLUES
230 730

They drove past the library.

They drove past the movie theater.

They drove past the barbershop.

None of them, not even Amelia, saw Bones.

They drove past the local coffeehouse.

The family drove nearly everywhere. But none of them, not even Amelia, saw Bones.

"Can we check at the animal shelter?" asked Amelia, who was starting to look like she might cry again.

Amelia's mother and father looked at each other.
They hadn't planned on checking there.

Before they entered the animal shelter, Amelia asked,
"Do you *promise* we can bring Bones home if he's there?"

"Oh, yes," said
Amelia's mother.

Amelia's father added,
"If we see Bones,
we'll bring him home."

Inside, there were a lot of dogs. They all began barking when they saw Amelia.

woof

woof

Amelia saw a yappy white dog like her grandma's.

woof

She saw a poofy black dog like the neighbor's.

woof

grrrr

She even saw a chunky yellow dog that looked rather like her school principal.

sniff

Then Amelia grinned.

"There he is! The small brown one with the wet pink nose! Do you see him?"

They did see a small brown dog with a wet pink nose.
In fact, they saw a lot of small brown dogs,
all with wet pink noses.

"Oh, yes," said Amelia's mother.

Amelia's father added,
"We see him."

But Amelia pointed to one in particular
as she hopped from one foot to the other.

"So we can take him home?" Amelia smiled.

She waited while a certain special small brown dog with a wet pink nose was led to them.

Amelia's father looked at Amelia's mother.

I thought we weren't ready for a dog.

Amelia's mother looked back at Amelia's father.

We may never be ready, but Amelia certainly is.

They both looked at Amelia and nodded.

"WE FOUND YOU!"

said Amelia loudly as she hugged the small brown dog with the wet pink nose.

Amelia whispered in his ear,

"And if anybody asks, your name is Bones."

Amelia's GUIDE TO GETTING YOUR **FIRST** DOG

in five EASY STEPS

1 Bones

PRETEND you have a dog

2 → LOST

LOSE your imaginary dog

#2